For André and Noelle

Library of Congress catalog card number: 2021935190
ISBN: 978-1-954980-94-5 (Paperback)
978-1-954980-95-2 (Hardback)

Formatting by Praise Saflor

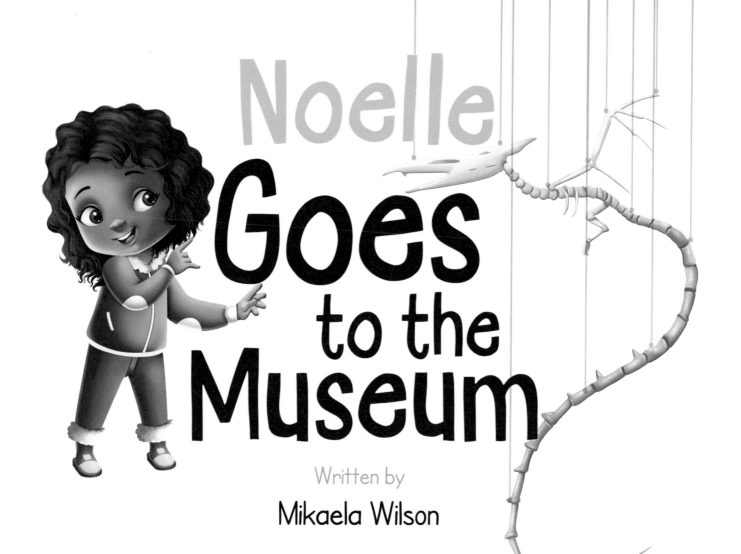

Noelle
Goes
to the
Museum

Written by

Mikaela Wilson

Illustrated by

Pardeep Mehra

Art Direction and Storyboards by

Mikaela Wilson

"No school today!" shouts Noelle, as she jumps out of bed. *"It's not a school day, so no learning today."*

"Noelle, would you like to learn about something fun today?" Mom asks.

"Learning isn't fun," says Noelle.

"What if you could learn about dinosaurs?" Mom asks. "Like the ones we read about in your dinosaur book!"

Noelle loves dinosaurs.
She grabs her jacket
and they hop in the car.

Soon Noelle sees a large building with lots of steps.
"We're here!" says Mom.

As they walk into the museum, Noelle sees huge dinosaur footprints on the floor.

Suddenly, Noelle hears a loud **GROWL**...
and an even louder **ROAR**.

"It's scary in here," Noelle whispers. "I don't want the dinosaurs to eat me!"

Noelle's mom kneels beside her.
"Don't worry, there's nothing to be scared of."

"The sounds are coming from the speakers," Mom says.

Noelle looks up at the speakers.
"*There's nothing to be scared of...*"

Suddenly, Noelle squeals with excitement.
"The dinosaurs are so **BIG!**"

TRICERATOPS
(try-SER-a-tops)

Meaning: "Three-horned face"
Length: 30 feet
Height: 10 feet
Weight: 5 tons (as much as a truck)
Diet: Plant eater (Herbivore)
Defense: Two long horns made of solid bone

"A **triceratops!**" Noelle shouts.

BRACHIOSAURUS
(brack-ee-uh-sau-rus)

Length: 85 feet
Height: 40-50 feet
Weight: 40 tons
Diet: Plant eater (Herbivore)
Defense: Size and long tail

"And there's a **brachiosaurus**.
It's as tall as this whole building!"

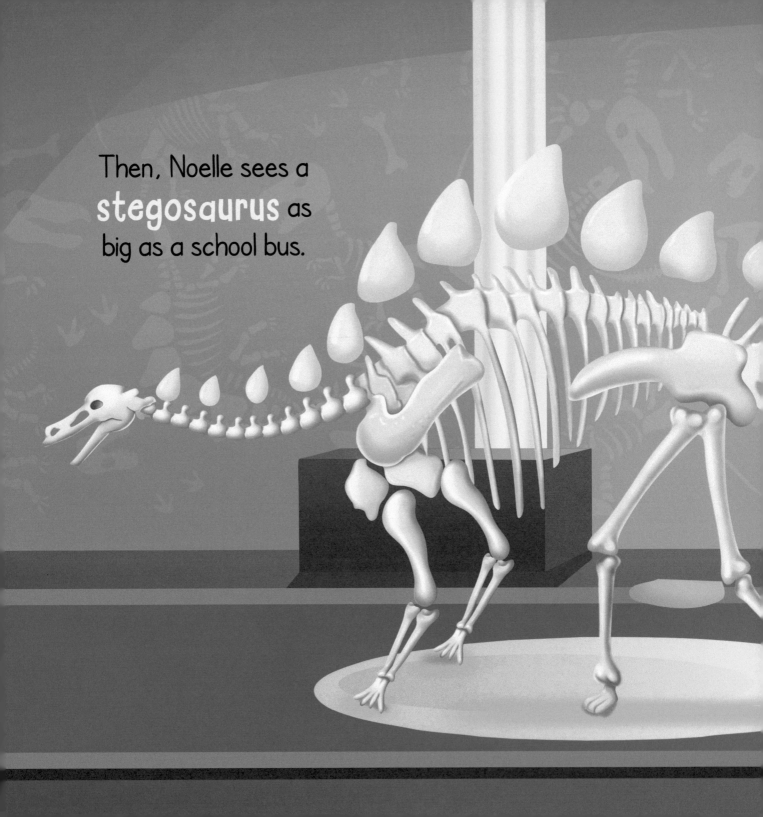

Then, Noelle sees a **stegosaurus** as big as a school bus.

When Noelle looks up, she sees a flying **pterodactyl**.

PTERODACTYL
(tear-uh-DACK-til)

STEGOSAURUS
(steg-uh-sau-rus)

Length: 21 feet
Height: 9 feet
Weight: 6 tons
Diet: Plant eater (Herbivore)
Defense: Spiked tail

Noelle walks over to the **velociraptor.**
"This dinosaur is the same size as me!"

VELOCIRAPTOR
(vuh-los-uh-rap-ter)

Length: 6 feet
Height: 2 feet
Weight: 4 pounds
Diet: Meat (Carnivore)
Defense: Claws

All of a sudden, Noelle turns around and sees...

...the gigantic Tyrannosaurus rex.
"Mom, it's the T-REX!
This is my favorite dinosaur!"

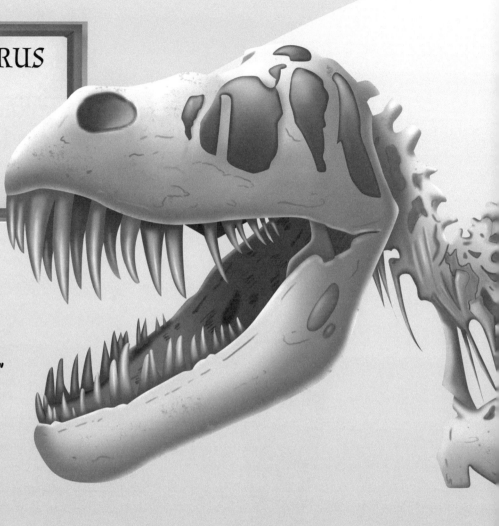

TYRANNOSAURUS REX
(tyran-no-sau-rus rex)

Length: 40 feet
Height: 12 feet
Weight: 8 tons
Diet: Meat (Carnivore)

"Look at all those sharp teeth! He sure looks scary!"

Noelle reaches out and holds Mom's hand. "Don't worry Mom, there's nothing to be scared of."

Noelle loves seeing
all the dinosaurs—
and learning so much.

Soon it's time to go home.

At dinner, Noelle talks about everything she learned at the museum.

That night as Mom tucks Noelle into bed, Noelle asks sleepily, "Mom, can we go back to the museum tomorrow? Learning really is fun."

André

Noelle

Dear Reader,

I hope you enjoyed reading this book!
If you have a moment to spare, please drop a quick
review on Amazon. I'm grateful for all the feedback!
If you have any questions or comments please email
mikaelawilsonbooks@gmail.com

Be the first to know about new book releases
and grab your free coloring pages at
www.mikaelawilsonbooks.com

 @mikaelawilsonbooks

 Mikaela Wilson Books

 @MikaelaWilsonBooks

About the Author
Mikaela Wilson

Mikaela Wilson is an author on a mission to bring fun, entertaining and meaningful stories to children's lives. In addition to working full-time as an IT Application Analyst, she is a wife and a mother of two young children. After reading countless children's books with her kids, she saw a need for more diversity in children's books and decided to create her own. The *André and Noelle* books are inspired by her two children and modeled after her own multicultural family. Mikaela hopes her books will be timeless and families can read and enjoy them for years to come.

About the Illustrator
Pardeep Mehra

Pardeep Mehra is the founder of Pencil Master Digital Studio, a family-owned business employing a large group of talented artists providing end-to-end illustration and publishing services. For more than 15 years, Pardeep has been providing his keen eye, visualization and digital art skills to create books that delight children all over the world. Pardeep lives in India with his wife and daughter. For more info visit www.pencilmasterdigi.com

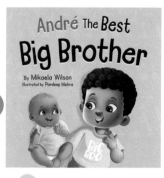

André The Best **Big Brother**
By Mikaela Wilson
Illustrated by Pardeep Mehra

Noelle The Best **Big Sister**
By Mikaela Wilson
Illustrated by Pardeep Mehra

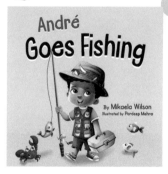

André **Goes Fishing**
By Mikaela Wilson
Illustrated by Pardeep Mehra

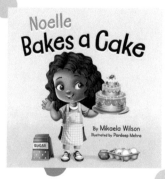

Noelle **Bakes a Cake**
By Mikaela Wilson
Illustrated by Pardeep Mehra

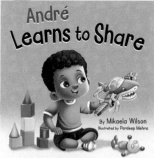

André **Learns to Share**
By Mikaela Wilson
Illustrated by Pardeep Mehra

Noelle **Goes to the Museum**
By Mikaela Wilson
Illustrated by Pardeep Mehra

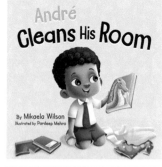

André **Cleans His Room**
By Mikaela Wilson
Illustrated by Pardeep Mehra

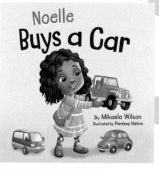

Noelle **Buys a Car**
By Mikaela Wilson
Illustrated by Pardeep Mehra

André and the **Special Gift**
By Mikaela Wilson
Illustrated by Pardeep Mehra

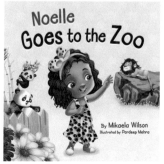

Noelle **Goes to the Zoo**
By Mikaela Wilson
Illustrated by Pardeep Mehra

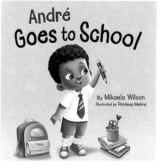

André **Goes to School**
By Mikaela Wilson
Illustrated by Pardeep Mehra

Noelle **Goes on a Picnic**
By Mikaela Wilson
Illustrated by Pardeep Mehra

Noelle and the **Haunted House**
By Mikaela Wilson
Illustrated by Pardeep Mehra

Scan the QR Code to find these titles and more!

MIKAELA WILSON BOOKS

Made in United States
Troutdale, OR
11/28/2023